The Big Ideas Club Presents

Living Myths

Revisiting Ancient Greece

Wolfish Rage II:

The Man is Sick

By

Jason Kassel, PhD

© 2025

Recursive Publishing

Part IV: The Man is Sick

Horrors of this Day

The group of twenty old men, strong warriors who saved the land of Thebes, weep and moan for Hercules. One turns to another. "When Danaus' fifty daughters murdered their husbands in Argos, that was unbelievable and thought to be Greece's most famous murder."

The fifty Danaids! No! Those women used their father's sword to chop their newly married husband's heads off! Ovid says the Danaids are punished in Hades like Sysyphus, except the women draw water into running tubes which spill eternally.

"The horrors of this day, though, surpass even those."

"Procne slew one of Zeus' sons as a blood sacrifice for the Muses. But Hercules has murdered three sons."

Procne! Demosthenes said she fed her own child to her husband for raping her sister! How could Hercules, son of Zeus and savior of Thebes, be compared to such villains?

"Wretched parent."

"You killed your children in a fate sent frenzy. What sighs, groans, or wails am I to raise? What dirges, what songs of Hades shall I sing?"

The twenty old men hear the doors to Hercules' home open and see the corpses of Megara and her three sons.

"Look there!"

"Look how the poor children are lying there dead!"

"Murdered by their own unfortunate father!"

The old men help bring the corpses into the courtyard. Old men come out of the inside of Hercules' crashed house.

"Look how he lies there, asleep!

"Look!"

"Look, what dreadful sleep after this dreadful murder!"

They group together in order to pull the bound Hercules from the inside and into the courtyard. He is asleep, encircled in strong rope from his shoulders to his legs, and attached to two broken pillars.

"Look at the amount of rope he's tied with!"

"Look at how thick the ropes are!"

"Look at how tightly Hercules is held to the stone pillars of his house!"

The old men look up to see Amphitryon emerge from the rubble of Hercules' home. The old warriors look at their friend and see his suffering.

"Look, Amphitryon, our old friend!"

"He wails like a mother bird who grieves for newborn featherless chicks."

"Look at his bitter steps, how slowly his feet move toward us."

Speak Softly, Old Theban Friends

There is my son, Hercules, son of Zeus. His body is strongly bound to those two pillars.

The group of twenty old hiplote warriors throw their arms around one another and crowd Amphitryon. They have left aside all of their warrior ethos. They cry and wail for his son, Hercules, son Zeus. He looks into their eyes. His own are blurry with tears and he is unable to see his friends' faces. "Let's speak softly, old Theban friends." He holds friends and they rub one another affectionately on the back. "Let Hercules sleep so he can forget his misery."

The old captain, a man of command, steps forward and throws his arms around Amphitryon. "I cry, weep, and mourn for you, old friend."

"For you and the children, too." The old sergeant joins his life-long comrades in an affectionate embrace.

An old man walks around the courtyard and looks at the rubble from what had been Zeus' altar in front of Hercules' home. "I cry for the man, your son, who was glorious in victory."

He sees a large group of men forming together around his son Hercules and he quickly rushes over. He protectively moves through the crowd and places himself between them and Hercules bound body. "Stand further back, old friends. Don't make any noise or outcry. Speak quietly and don't wake the poor man from his calm, peaceful sleep."

Another group of old men are looking inside what remains of Hercules' destroyed home. They are loudly discussing the gore inside. "Look at all that blood and slaughter."

He hears them, his head hurts, and his heart moves fast. "Stop! Quiet! You will be my ruin!"

The group of old men either don't hear or don't care. "Look, the slaughter he has split rises against him."

He leaves Hercules' bound body and rushes to their side. "Cry softly, old friends! Gently raise your dirge of woe, old friends. If he wakes, and bursts his bonds, he may destroy the city." He pleads with them not to wake his son Hercules.

He'll kill me, his father, and then smash the whole palace to pieces.

He is Dead Asleep

Twenty old warrior men are scattered around the courtyard with their eyes full of tears and their arms resting on one another's backs. Two men stand embracing. One is urging the other to remain faithful and pray to Zeus.

"I can not!" He cries. "I can not!"

Their poor, suffering old friend, Amphitryon, who told everyone he had been cuckolded by Zeus. They grieve for his losses. A group of old men have gathered around him. He stands in front of them and Hercules and waves his arms. "Hush, old friends. Let me note his breathing. I will put my ear close and listen."

The group of old men run backwards. "Is he asleep?"

Old Amphitryon has his ear pressed against Hercules' chest and the old men watch as their friend's face changes. "Yes, he's dead asleep." He stands, embraces the eyes of each old comrade, and breaks down in tears. "After murdering his wife and children with the arrows of his twanging bow."

The group of twenty old men crowd and collect around Amphitryon. Their bodies collect together, create warmth, and establish unity. "Grieve, then, Amphitryon!"

Amphitryon has collapsed onto the ground. He is no longer recognizable and is inconsolable. "I am grieving!"

The group of twenty old men nod in unison. There is so much for their friend to moan, groan, and cry about. "Old man, grieve the poor children."

"My grandchildren." Amphitryon faces the ruins of Zeus' altar.

"Grieve for your son, old friend!"

"My son!" His wail can be heard down the cliff in the city of Thebes below.

The old captain turns to the old sergeant. "My poor, old friend!" The two old men embrace and their cheeks meet the other's shoulder.

One old man after another changes their body posture until all twenty, and Amphitryon, have become tense. They have all become aware of Hercules twitching and turning.

His father turns to the group of old men. "Hush! Hush!" He turns his head and the twenty old men see wide white eyeballs, raised eyebrows, and a creased brow. "He is turning! He is waking up!" Their old friend rises with speed. "I better hide myself beneath the roof of that house."

An old man, who had kept quiet until now, steps forward. He wants to see the old Amphitryon, the one who was proud and would stand during a fight..

"Courage, old friend. Night still holds darkness in his shut eyes."

The father comes to him. "No, look. I am not afraid of dying." He has stopped his weeping, moaning, and groaning. "I am not afraid to leave the light of day after my miseries." He has regained his warrior composure and speaks as a young man who is not concerned about himself. "I fear that if he wakes up and kills me, his own father, it will add an evil upon another. The Furies will add the spilling of a parent's blood to their curse."

"It would have been better if you had died after your triumphant return." The group of old men remember the days of their youth when they returned from their victorious campaign over the kingdom of Pterelaus and they were celebrated by every Theban in the city. "You avenged your wife's brothers and sacked the sea encircled Taphian city." The old men chant a chorus of 'Hear! Hear!'

The old father places his old body in front of the bound body of Hercules tied to two pillars. He holds his arms long to the side and plants his feet. "Run away from here, old friends. Make haste from this palace and escape Hercules' fury." The sounds of a waking man cause the old father to tremble. "The maddened man wakes. He will soon heap more carnage and add more murders on the old." The old father has lost his warrior memory. He falls to the ground, facing his old comrades, and weeps. "The whole of Thebes will be in a frenzy as he rages wildly through the streets."

The group of twenty old men raise their faces to the sky and speak in unison. "Oh Zeus, why do you show such savage hate against your own son? Why have you plunged him into such a sea of troubles?"

I am Confused and Distraught

His eyes move from side to side behind closed lids. His jaw lowers, he breathes through his mouth, and his tongue wets his lips. He shakes his head. *Ah! I am breathing, yes I am alive.* He opens his eyes. *My eyes see everything I should see.* He uses his sense of reason. *I see the sky, the earth, and the sun's brilliant shafts.* He can't remember where he is or how he has gotten here. *But my senses reel, and it's as if I've fallen into a tempest.* This isn't like waking up from a dream or even a nightmare. *My mind has plunged in a dreadful turbulence.* There is a physical difference. His body has become transformed. *My breath is feverishly hot and flows out of my lungs in quick spasms.*

Aware of being unaware, he becomes aware of his physical surroundings. *What?* He identifies his location. *How?* He recognizes his predicament. *Why am I lying here with my youthful arms and chest tied fast?* Craning his neck, he comprehends his bondage. *Why do ropes like a ship's cables tie me to this smashed and shattered colum.one?*

His limbs restrained, his body neutered with rope, he struggles and uses his head and neck to assist his eyes. His breath increases, sweat pours from his brow, and his breath quickens. Until, in the very left corner of his eye - *Look on the floor over there.*

Unable to loosen the ropes, his strong body tied to the smashed columns, he sees a sight that strangles his heart as tightly as the ropes strangle his body. The corner of his left eye sees his best friends, his family's loyal allies, and his comrade-in-arms. *My bow and my poor arrows - my arms' worthy companions and squires - lie scattered.* The friends he brought with him into war, that helped him defeat his enemies, and that watched over him as a friend. *Arrows that have protected my flanks and kept me safe.* His body neutered and emasculated with rope, his eyes fill with tears which steam down his cheeks. *They kept me safe and they were kept safe by me.* His left eye strains. *Look at my arrows scattered everywhere.*

He is weeping, lacks sense, and feels utterly abandoned by his only comrades-in-arms. He is unable to move or loosen his restraints even a bit. The only body part he has full control over is his head. He feels his bowels release. *Have I gone back down and come back up from Hades' halls?* He tries to use his reason and memory. *I just returned on the journey for Eurystheus. No. I do not see Sisyphos with his rock. Nor do I see Pluto or his queen - Demeter's child - Persephone.*

Neutered, emasculated, bound except for his neck and head, and bereft of the only battle friend he's known, a realization washes over his body. *I am confused and distraught.* He is aware, he has a sense, a feeling, an intuition that his mind should be more than it is. *I cannot remember where I am.*

He remembers he has the power of speech. He shifts his neck and rotates his head. His eyes spot an old man. "You there. Do I have a friend nearby?" His eyes only see the old man's general shape. His ears do not hear any response. He speaks more loudly. "Can a friend help me understand and end my ignorance? I have no knowledge of things once familiar."

His ears hear sounds but he can't make out their meaning. Then he hears Amphitryon, his father, speak. "Old friends, what do you say? Should I approach the destructive scene of my sorrow?"

He hears the voice of his father's old captain. "Yes. I'll come with you. I won't abandon or desert you in your hour of trouble."

Neutered and emasculated, he can only move his neck and head. He hears his father weep and moan. "Father, what's wrong?" His eyes watch the sky above and his ears hear old men in the courtyard. Inside their sockets, he turns his eyes far to the right until his father comes into view. "Why do you weep with tears?" He tries to make out his father's face but his eyes are too strained and his father is too distant. "Why veil your eyes from me? Why do you stand so far from me? I am your beloved son."

He weeps as his bondage denies him the ability to use his body, his weapon is scattered and unable to assist, and his father won't look or approach his neutered and emasculated body.

I am the son you love so dearly.

If Your Senses Have Recovered

His poor son, Hercules, son of Zeus. Everything has been taken from him. Zeus has abandoned his son. He looks into his eyes to force his love through the window and into Hercules' soul. "My son, yes." He moves closer, smells his son's fear, and collapses on the ground. "My child." He throws himself over his son's bound body. "Even after causing such disaster and misery, you are my son and child." Lying on his bound son, he inhales his weakness.

His son becomes still and no longer tries to struggle against the ropes. "Disaster?" His son exhales and he feels his abdomen lower. He hears his son's heartbeat quicken. "What calamity have I caused to make you so sad you weep and cry?" His son's muscles tense and he feels him go to war with his bounds.

Afraid, he jumps off and backs away. Then he comes to realize the ropes have bound him completely and his son is unable to move. He inhales and chooses his words. "My son, if a god suffered this disaster, and found out, the god would weep and cry."

Please, Zeus! Don't make me breathe the air that will have to say the words.

His son turns his head as looks at him through a small tilted black hole. "Father, that is a bold and terrible thing to assert." His son struggles without hope against the rope that binds him to the two smashed columns. "You haven't explained what disaster I caused you." His son's strong arms are tense and struggling but the rope does not budge.

Please, Zeus! My old lungs do not have the power to heal my son's pain.

He runs to his son's side, places himself on top of his son, looks down, and his own tears drip onto his son's face. "My son, if your senses have recovered, and you are restored, then your own eyes see the disaster."

His son's body stills. His face goes blank and then his eyes close. His look becomes neither angry nor happy nor sad. He doesn't struggle or attempt to act. His face is calm and he waits to hear his fate. "Father, no more riddles. Sketch the scene and explain."

His son's eyes have reopened and stare at him intently. He realizes his son's reason is only partially regained. "I will explain once I'm sure your mind has recovered and you aren't mad as a fiend of hell."

His son doesn't appreciate hearing this and he begins struggling against the ropes. Afraid for himself, and his old friends, and the city of Thebes, he steps back until he is sure Hercules' eye can't follow.

He watches his son struggle against the ropes in vain and scream into the sky asking his father for help. "Tell me!" His poor, strong son is unable to use his muscles to free himself. He is unable to even move. All that he can do is shout into the sky. "What new life disasters do these dark suspicious hints represent?"

He weeps and rushes to his son's side. He is afraid. He leans over his bound son, places his mouth against his ear, and speaks in a voice above a whisper. "I will but I don't know if you have sober senses." He moves his head to see into his son's eyes. Still in a voice above a whisper. "Do you still remain in the grips of Hades' madness?"

His son's body stills and his eyes go wide. "I don't remember being mad!"

He moves away from his bound son. He walks around the courtyard, shakes his head, scratches his beard. He looks at the twenty old men. "Old friends, shall I loosen and undo my son's ropes? Tell me, what should I do?"

I Feel Shame

Hercules' breast swells with angry air, his muscles strain against the thick ropes, and his face reddens. His face focused on the sky above, sees his father Zeus and screams at Amphitryon. "Yes, loosen and undo my ropes." Struggling against the ropes, he feels the shame of emasculation. He wants vengeance against those who put him in such a womanly situation. "Say the name of who bound and tied me." He struggles against the ropes but is unable to move even an inch. He continues to rage. "I feel shame to be treated this way."

Why is father acting in such a shameful way?

He smells his father approach, lean over his body, and reveal his face. His eyes are red, tears flow into his beard and down his cheeks, and his nose empties phlegm.

Why won't he release me? Why is he shaming me?

"This shame is enough."

Why does he look at me like that? He doesn't feel the blood he's released through his struggling.

"Rest content."

Father, free me! Blood covers Hercules' body.

"You don't need to know about your troubles. Forget the rest." His father places his hand on Hercules' blood-covered chest.

He sees his Amphitryon's eyes and screams at Zeus. "Enough of this." He lifts his head as far as his neck will allow. He tightens his eyes and demands. "My silence won't provide the answer. Tell me what happened to me."

Why did he step out of the air through which my eyes receive vision? Oh Zeus! The shame to my thumos. Why can't I free myself?

After a few moments of time, during which he continues to struggle and bleed, he hears his father's voice from a distance. "Oh Zeus, in your throne up there seated next to Hera, can you see these deeds proceeding?"

Hera! Oh Zeus! What now?

Hercules ceases his struggles and his breathing slows. "Have I suffered from her enmity?"

There is no answer.

Why won't my father speak? Hera has returned? It was meant to end after my twelve labors!

He struggles against the ropes, bleeds, and screams helplessly and shamefully into the air. He excoriates his father Zeus. "Hera attacked me?"

His father shows his face. His eyes are red, spread wide, and he smells of fear. "Come now, a truce with the goddess."

Truce! What has she done! Release me!

His father's voice pleads. "Leave her alone. Take care of your own troubles."

He stops struggling and breathes. He takes in air and holds it inside his breast for two heartbeats. He then releases the air and waits for two more heartbeats. "I am undone." His eyes, which had been filled with rage, are replaced with eyes filled with fear. "I am destroyed." His eyes are filled with eleos. "A disaster will unfold I must endure."

His father's eyes widen and his mouth drops agape. "My son, look at the bodies."

Look? I can't move!

"See your children's corpses."

Hera has attacked my children?

His mouth forms words but his mind is unraveling. "Oh horror! What hideous sight is here?" *What has Hera done to my sons?* "What sorrow is this?" *What does the goddess continue to torment and punish me? When is enough enough? When do my labors end?*

His father's face has disappeared and he hears his words. My son, against your sons you waged an unnatural war."

I waged war?

Staring at the sky he sees and speaks to his father Zeus. "What do you mean? Say who killed these children."

His father's face returns and his eyes see one of his arrows with blood on the tip. "You and your arrows, my son." His father's face, and the arrow, disappear but not before a drop of the blood dropped onto his chest. "And a god brought it all about."

He can only see his father Zeus in the sky above. He speaks to Zeus, to Amphitryon, to anyone who will listen. "Father, what are you saying? What have I done? Speak as the messenger of evil news."

His father's face appears. His eyes red, tears flowing, phlegm falling, his poisonous words hang in the air. "I am saying, my son, you went distraught and, in a fit of madness, killed your sons." Hercules screams into the sky, struggles helplessly against, and weeps. His father's voice comes from afar. "Your questions receive sad answers."

Lament and Groan

Amphitryon looks at his son Hercules, son of Zeus and weeps. His strong and powerful son, bound in rope, and bleeding is helpless. The sound of his son's voice is frightening. "Have I also murdered my wife?" He can't look at his son. He turns his back and walks away to create distance. He bows his head and waves his hand.

"Yes. All this, Hercules, is the work of your own unaided hand."

His son doesn't make a sound. He is no longer weeping or struggling against the ropes. He can't bear to look at his strong son, so helpless and in such pain. His son's voice sounds of agony. "Woe is me. I'm wrapped in a cloud of sorrow and surrounded by sighs and groans."

He rushes to his son's side, places his hands on his bound and bloody shoulders, and looks into his eyes. "I lament and groan for the fate you suffer, my son." His son's eyes are full of tears.

"Did I dash my house to pieces in my frenzy?"

His tears fall onto his son's bound body. "I only know that your life is undone and you are ruined." There is silence as the two stare at one another. He stands over his son gazing into his eyes and his hand resting on his strong bound shoulder.

Oh, my poor son Hercules, son of Zeus. Why does such pain happen to me?

His son's eyes transform from black to aware. "Where was I when my frenzied madness seized me and destroyed my life?" His voice sounds stronger and he begins struggling with his rope.

He looks at his son and then turns his back and walks away. "In the moment it seized you, you were standing by the altar, and purifying your hands with the fire."

Why Did I Not Murder Myself?

Bound and bleeding on the two smashed columns, Hercules is emasculated without power. His bow and his arrows lie scattered outside his sight. He cries. He struggles against the ropes but to no avail.

Why did I not murder myself?

He shouts at his father Zeus in the heavens in the sky above. "Why murder my darling sons and spare my own life?"

Agghh. I hate myself!

His father Zeus, in the heavens above, is silent. He rages. "Should I not go and leap or hurl myself off some sheer cliff? Should I dig my sword into my entrails?"

Why am I alive? I serve no purpose.

He struggles against the rope, continues to bleed, and screams hopelessly into the empty sky above. "Should I aim the sword against my heart to bring justice and avenge my children's blood?"

I hate everything about myself! Why am I alive!

Since his father Zeus won't answer his angry screams he begins to beg for mercy. "Should I throw my flesh onto a pyre? Burn my body in the fire to escape the life of hatred and infamy that now awaits me?"

As he wails against his fortune he notices a bird fly pass and he turns his head. From the very far corner of his eye, he sees a familiar shape that transforms his emotions. From the depths of his despair, his reason returns, and he finds hope.

Before I practice my plans to die, I have a new hurdle to jump. Theseus, my friend and relative, is coming.

His only thoughts are for his friend's health. "The eyes of my dearest friend will become polluted if he sees me as a murderer of own children." If the murders pollute his eyes, lead into his blood, and through his blood into his thoughts, he would harm Theseus. This thought causes him more pain than emasculating helplessness against the rope binding him to the two smashed columns.

What can I do now?

He closes his eyes. His reason is overcome with feelings of shame. The utter hopelessness of his bound emasculation and disgust with himself returns. *Where can I find release from my sorrow and escape this grief? Should I take wings and soar to the heavens or sink and plunge down beneath the earth?*

All he wants to do is become invisible. In his bound and emasculated position he devises a plan - *I'll veil my head in the darkness of my cloak.* - and shifts his head so his cloak covers his face. Now, he is blind while bound to the two smashed columns. He can't allow his friend to see his face. *I am ashamed.* His thoughts revolve in circles. *The shame of the blood-*

guiltiness I have done to my children is too great. More than anything, he wants to spare his friend any pain or harm. What he has done is so horrible, he can't allow a friend to see. *If I were to let an innocent man's eyes fall on me, the innocent could be harmed for my sin of spilling blood.*

Part V: A Healthy Hero Returns

A Piteous Prelude

Theseus walks into the courtyard accompanied by five hoplite soldiers. All of them have healthy good looks, are broad shouldered, and their long hair flows in the outside breeze. He arrives in the courtyard with a wide and happy smile but his expression changes as he sees the rubble of Hercules' home. Looking around the courtyard, he sees the twenty old men, and then his eyes settle on Amphitryon. His eyes widen and he smiles. "Old friend, I have arrived with young Athenian warriors." He gestures to the five hoplites, then points down but away from Thebes below. "Armed and encamped, we are waiting by the streams of Asopos. We have arrived to help Hercules, your son." He walks around the ruins of Hercules' home and scratches his head.

He stands straight, walks toward Amphitryon, and speaks with seriousness. "The city of Athena received a rumor from Erecheis that Lukos usurped this city, became your enemy, and waged war against you." Theseus embraces Amphitryon. "When I heard Hercules needed help, I came to make recompense for his kind deed. He saved me from the underworld." He gestures and calls for his five hoplites to join his side. "If needed, I and my allies are here to provide aid."

He looks around, lifts his chin, and points. "But what is this heap of dead?" He walks around the courtyard and inspects the rubble that was Hercules' home. "The ground is already covered in corpses. Am I too late? Did a delay fail to stop new disasters?" He bends and lowers himself to inspect the bodies lying in the rubble of Hercules' home. "Who murdered these children?" He walks to each of the bodies and looks closely. He sees Megara's corpse, stands, and looks quizzically at Amphitryon. "Whose wife is this here? Boys are not sent to battle or war." He turns toward his group of five hoplite soldiers, shakes his head, and speaks with utter sadness. "I must be discovering another type of disaster."

Amphitryon's face is lowered to the ground, his eyes look at his feet, and shame rises in his head. "Lord Theseus, from the land of olive trees."

The greeting startles him. "Why this piteous prelude in addressing me?" He expected praise, garlands, and gestures of love.

What has happened to the home of Hercules? Why is there a dead woman and children amidst all this rubble? Is Hercules lying there, bound and bloody, trying to hide his face? What in Zeus' name is happening to my friend?

Theseus walks directly to Amphitryon and lifts his head. He forces the old man to look him in the eyes and he tries to comprehend Amphitryon's words.

"The heavens have delivered and afflicted us great suffering, lord!"

He gestures at the surrounding rubble. "Whose children are these that you are weeping and grieving?"

Amphitryon pushes Theseus and runs to another part of the courtyard. "My own son's children, Theseus. My unfortunate son." The old man's back shakes as he wails and moans. "He was their father and butcher both." The old man collapses on the ground in tears. "His heart hardened when he did the bloody deed."

Theseus runs across the courtyard, lowers himself, and places a hand on Amphitryon's back. "What are you saying, Amphitryon?" He gestures at the rubble that was Hercules' home. "How did this happen?"

What Dreadful Things You Say

Amphitryon is too ashamed to face Theseus. He is shaking with sadness. "In a wild fit of frenzied madness, Hercules shot arrows dipped in the hundred-headed Hydra's blood.."

Theseus removes his hand. "Stop, Amphitryon." His voice sounds as if he's walked away. "Use good words."

He begins sobbing. "Oh, how I wish I could do that." His face forward, his teary and blurry eyes focused on the collapsed rubble of Hercules' home.

Theseus' voice is distant, as though he is at the other end of the courtyard. "What dreadful things you say."

He turns around and sees Theseus holding his palm to his mouth, shaking his head, and looking at Hercules' three dead sons. Theseus continues staring at the dead bodies for minutes until he doesn't and he makes eye contact with Amphitryon. The two share a gaze for two beats, Amphitryon inhales, and speaks with utter despair. "Fortune has spread her wings, and we are ruined. Gone. This is our end."

Theseus inhales. He shakes his head and mutters something that sounds like 'not the Hercules I know.' He looks into Amphitryon's eyes. "I see Hera's work." He gestures with his arm. "This is her carnage." Theseus walks around the rubble and sees Hercules, bound to two columns and bloody from his struggles, hiding his face. "Who is this man lying here among the corpses, old man?"

Amphitryon walks next to Theseus so he is at his side. "That is my son, the enduring warrior." He begins crying. "A son of many miseries who marched and fought with gods while killing giants on the plains of Phlegra."

Theseus places an arm on his back. "Woe for him. Was a mortal's fortune ever as cursed or caused a man to suffer so much?"

Amphitryon, comforted by Theseus touch, breaks into moans and groans. "Never will you find another mortal who has borne a larger share of suffering, been more fatally deceived, or who has been so tortured as he."

The two men stand in awe of the sufferings the gods have bestowed on Hercules' shoulders. After several minutes, Theseus turns to Amphitryon. "Why does he veil his head with his cloak?"

Amphitryon shakes his head and turns away. "Your kind intent makes him ashamed to meet your eyes." He sobs and shakes. "The shame of facing you after murdering his sons is too great."

In the midst of his sobbing, he hears Theseus. "Uncover his head. I have come to sympathize and share in his grief."

Why can't they both just leave me be? I don't want to see or speak with anyone. I hate myself. I want to die. How could I have killed my own sons?

I Don't Speak In Hand Gestures

Hands are grabbing at his ropes and he hears his mortal father's voice. "Son, pull away that cover from your eyes." As the restraints are loosened, he breathes deeply. "Let the sun see your face." As the rope is unwound, his head stays hidden behind his cloak. "It is a hard task to stand up against one's tears." His father speaks directly into the cloth covering his face and he smells his breath. "My aged eyes shed tears. I grasp your beard, your knees, and your hands. I beg you, my child." He moves his head to the right to keep it covered. "Restrain your savage lion's temper. Don't use it against yourself. You are rushing forth across a path of unholy bloodshed, eager to add one woe upon another."

Just leave me alone. I don't want to speak to anyone. I don't want to be with anyone. I don't want to be, period. Just leave me alone. Let me die. Why won't I die? Oh Zeus! Why is this happening? Why did I kill my own sons? I am your son. Why is this happening to me?

Theseus and Amphitryon don't make a sound for several minutes. After that, a person's foot kicks him. He hears Theseus. "Hey, you." He stirs faintly. He hears a laugh. "Yes, you. Lying down there, huddled in the depths of your misery. I am calling you." The last of his restraints are removed and he has regained control of all his limbs. "Come and show your face to your friends."

He grabs his hood in shame and closes it around his face. "The darkest blackness wouldn't hide the pains of this catastrophe." He struggles against

Theseus but eventually sees the light in the courtyard. Theseus is directly in front of him, his father stands behind him, and his son's bodies are on his right. He starts to speak, then raises his hand, points, sobs, and tries to close the cloak around his face.

"I don't speak in hand gestures." Theseus grabs his hands. "Are you trying to say something about murder?" His hands are pulled apart and he sees the light of the sun. "Are you afraid to pollute me with your words? It doesn't matter to me, Hercules. So what if I suffer and share your fate."

He sees Theseus' bright smile and open arms. "Whatever good fortune I have began the day you removed me from the dark of death and brought me to the light of life." He accepts Theseus' embrace. "I hate a friend whose gratitude grows old." He unburdens as Theseus rubs his back. "It is a terrible man who sails in a friend's happy moments but is unwilling to share the ship of poor fortune with him."

Theseus lifts him. "Arise, Hercules and uncover your poor face." He sits up with his back straight. "Look at me, you poor wretch." He stares at the rubble that was his home and the bodies that were his sons and wife. "The noble gallant soul accepts and endures, without a word, the death blows sent by the gods."

I See The Horrible Sight

Theseus smiles as he embraces his friend. Being near his friend, and knowing that he can help, brings him immense joy. His happiness at seeing his friend has erased the reality of the horrors that surround the courtyard. He helps Hercules, who has rope in piles around his lower body, sit straight in the middle of rubble between two smashed columns. He places his hands on Hercules' shoulders and grabs his robe to cover the bleeding wounds.

Hercules stares at him with empty eyes. "Theseus, can you witness and see my children's torture?"

He speaks! Oh, Zeus, thank you for bringing me to my friend! Thank you for letting me see his face and hear his voice.

Theseus stands above him and warmly rubs Hercules' shoulder. "Yes, I have heard of them." He squeezes. "I see the horrible sight." He rubs and pats his friend's shoulder, attempting to transmit his feelings through touch.

His friend is dejected. "Then why did you unveil my head?" His voice sounds empty, hollow, and is full of despair. "Why did you let the sun see my face?"

Oh, Zeus! Thank you for allowing me to be close to my friend who saved me from Hades, the underworld below. Thank you for allowing me the opportunity to provide help and comfort to a friend.

Theseus lowers himself, he is eye-level with Hercules, and places his hands on Hercules' upper arms. "Why?" The friendly, brotherly, loving feelings inside him emerge into the air in words. "Hercules. you are a mortal." He rubs his friend's arms. "Mortals cannot pollute that which belongs to the gods." He looks into his eyes and attempts to transmit his feelings of love.

Hercules pushes him away, grabs his cloak, and covers his face. "Fly away." He speaks behind his robe. "Leave this luckless wretch alone." Theseus hears him weep. "Leave this place of sin." Theseus hears more weeping. "I have blemished it with my unholy taint." Hercules sobs, moans, and groans.

Theseus stands and looks at the old men in the courtyard. Then he looks at the hoplites he brought. He leans over and tries to get Hercules to stand. "Hercules, vengeance may be a fiend but it doesn't travel from friend to friend."

Hercules stares into the distance and doesn't move his body. "That's true, Theseus." He nods his head. "I have no regret for the good deed and service I did you." Theseus feels Hercules' tense body relax a bit.

Ah! He recognizes friendship. Good.

He rubs his friend's arms. "In thanks, I give you my sympathy." He looks into his friend's eyes. "I show my pity."

Hercules swats him away. "Sympathy?" He spits the word. "Pity?" From his mouth, the word sounds dirty. "I deserve this for murdering my sons?"

Theseus looks down on his friend and smiles. "Yes, Hercules." He squeezes his shoulder. "I weep for your changed fortunes."

I've Resolved To Die

Hercules' eyes, cloudy with tears, stare at the rubble that was his home, the bodies that were his sons, and the body that was his wife. He weeps and moans. "Like no other man, I am afflicted with suffering misfortunes." He places his head in his hands and cries.

Oh, Zeus, my father from the heaven's above. Why do you keep me alive? Why won't you let me die? How can you allow someone like me to live? Someone who is capable of killing his own sons and the woman he loves? That type of person shouldn't be on earth. Oh, I wish I could die.

Weeping into his hands, he feels the warmth of his friend's hand on his back. In between his sobbing and sniffing, he hears his friend's voice. "Hercules, your misfortunes stretch from the earth to the heavens."

Exactly!

He nods his head and turns to look at his friend's face. "And that's why I've resolved to die."

That is the only answer. How can I go on living after committing such an act as this? What a horrible human being I am. What kind of man kills his sons?

His friend's slaps, on his left and right cheeks, are hard. "How would that help?" Another slap on his right cheek. "Do you think the gods care about such threats?" And another on his left.

He grabs his friend's wrist and stops a third slap. "The heavens have been remorseless and the gods arrogant." He releases his friend's wrist. "I shall act in kind." He prepares to stand.

"Hold your tongue, Hercules." His friend wears a shocked expression. "Your presumptuous words could bring you even more pain and suffering." His friend shakes his head and frowns.

The gods? More? What more can the gods do to me?

Standing, his torso bloody and bleeding, he lowers his head and waves at the surrounding rubble and bodies. "My ship is freighted with pains of sorrow." His head moves from left to right over the rubble and dead bodies. He covers his face with his hands and cries. "I have no room or space to stow anything more."

His hands over his face he sees anything. Mucus fills his nostrils and breathing is hard. He can barely hear his friend's words. "What are you going to do?" His friend's fists hit his chest. "How far will your anger take you?

He removes his hands from his face and stares into his friend's eyes. "I will die again and return to the world below from where I have come." He tears, cries, and sobs. "I will return to Hades, the Underworld."

Mortals Have Never Helped Me

Theseus punches his friend's chest and slaps his face. He grabs his friend's face and stares into his eyes. "Hercules, you use the words of a common person." He shakes his head in disgust.

Hercules' eyes widen, he looks at his friend, and he waves his arms to show the rubble and corpses in the courtyard. "You speak without knowing my grief and your advice is outside sorrow's pale, Theseus." His friend's eyes well with tears. His friend cries.

Oh, Zeus! Who is this man in front of me? Is this the man that went to Hades and rescued me from the underworld?

He stands and slaps his friend. Hard. He turns to the old men in the courtyard. "Are these the words of the much-endured mighty Hercules?" He backhand slaps him. Hard.

Hercules stands but doesn't move. He stares at the rubble that was his home and points to his sons' bodies. "I have endured but this is too much." His friend's body shakes, crumbles, and collapses. "Endurance must come in moderation." His friend is on his knees, his upper torso bleeding, and his arms raised to the sky. "Endurance must have a limit." He sobs, wails, and moans.

Oh, Zeus! What has happened to the friend who rescued me?

He moves away from the fallen and broken Hercules. He looks around the courtyard and sees the frightened old men of Thebes. He shakes his head and feels shame. "I am speaking with Hercules, the mighty benefactor and ally of mortals?" He looks at the Athenian hoplites. He brought these men with him to help his friend. He frowns.

My friend has disappeared. He has been replaced with this?

His friend's voice is weak, feeble, and whiny. "Mortals have never helped me." Pouty. "Hera has her way." He cries. "She controls all this." His arms continue to wave at the rubble that was his home and the bodies that were his family.

What has happened to the man who rescued me? Where is my friend?

He stands above and behind his friend. Immediately in front of them is the rubble that was the altar of Zeus. All around them is the rubble that was Hercules' home. He places his hand on Hercules' shoulder and squeezes flesh that is covered with dirt, dried mucus, and dried blood. "Greece will never allow Hercules to die such a perverse and mindless death." He feels a shift in his friend's body, lets go of his shoulder, and walks two steps backward.

His friend pauses for a second, then stands, turns, and he is confronted with a feverish face. Hercules has red eyes full of tears and a mustache and beard covered in mucus. His index finger pounds the air as he speaks.

He has the mania. Listen to the words he uses. What happened to the man who brought me up from the darkness and into the light?

His friend's red eyes are wide open, he uses the back of his hand to rub mucus from his mustache, and he spits words into the air. "Hear me! Listen! I will use reason! I will list with words why my death will not be mindless."

Who is he trying to reason with? Himself? He has become two people. He has the mania!

"Listen and I will unfold the reasons." Hercules sniffs away his tears. "I will explain why, both in the past and now, I have found my life unbearable."

At least he's no longer crying. I feel such shame seeing this man. Where is my friend who rescued me? The man who saved me from Hades, the world below.

"Let me start with my birth." His friend speaks rapidly and loudly. "I was born to a father who had the stained guilt of bloodshed." His friend stabs with his index finger. "Before he married my mother, he murdered his old father-in-law." His friend widens his eyes and raises his eyebrows. "When a race is born of badly laid foundations, all descendants are fated to live a cursed and miserable life." His friend hunches over, shakes, and cries.

Where is the son of Zeus? Where is the half-mortal that descended and ascended from the underworld below?

Forget About My Labors

Hercules' thoughts are racing.

I hate myself so much! I wish I would die! Oh Zeus, why do you keep me alive?

His eyes blurry, his nose running, spittle flies out of his mouth. "Then Zeus," he inhales and stares at the rubble that was his house and the bodies that were his family, "whoever this Zeus might be," his waves dismissively at the rubble that was Zeus' altar, "begot me so I would be the focus of Hera's hatred."

That cruel woman! My only crime was being born. She punishes me for a crime I didn't commit. Why is she so hateful?

He feels a hand on his shoulder, turns, and sees a weeping Amphitryon. Staring into his fearful eyes, he understands the impact of his words, slows, and inhales. He speaks from his heart to Amphitryon's eyes. "Don't be upset. I regard you as my true father and not Zeus." He walks away from his father and toward the bodies that used to be his family.

He cries in despair. "While still a breastfeeding baby, Hera sent fierce snakes into my cradle to kill me." He faces the sky in misery. "After I grew to become a man, and firm flesh covered my young body, I performed the labors." He raises his voice in anger. "What is the point of talking about them all now?" He points in the direction of the rubble that was his home. "Why talk about the lions? The three-bodied Typhons? The giants?"

He stares at an old man in the courtyard and begins to mumble. "Forget about the battle against an army of four legged Centaurs." His upper body crumbles. "Forget the hydra, that beast with the many heads that kept growing back." He walks in a circle and cries into the sky above. "I performed countless tasks before ending in the Underworld where I obeyed Eurystheus' command and brought the three-headed dog up to the light of the sun."

With one hand, he points at the rubble that was his home. His other hand points at the bodies that were his family. "This bloody deed is my last labor I perform." He brings both hands to his face. "I crowned the sorrows and miseries of my house with my own sons' murder." He speaks into his hands. "I have arrived at such a sorry state."

He sobs into his hands for minutes and then speaks with his face raised toward the sky above. "I love the city of Thebes, but piety requires that I leave." He begins mumbling. "No longer may I dwell in the city I love." He lowers his face to the ground. He mumbles. "If I did stay, which temple or to what friends could I turn?" He kicks dirt. "No friendly greetings or invitations will follow the horror of my curse." He begins to cry.

"I can't go to Argos, because I'm an exile from my own country." He covers his face and continues mumbling. "Another city, perhaps? But, which one?" He paces and mumbles. "And even if there is a city that will take me," he kicks dirt, "I don't think I could endure the sneers," he paces, "the painful jabs," he mumbles, "the bitter tongues," he cries, "all thrown at men with a bad name." He turns and looks at an old man. "I can hear them all say, 'Oh look, that is Zeus' son who killed his wife and sons. Why doesn't he get the hell out of our land?'" He falls to his knees and wails.

A hand touches his shoulder, he sees it belongs to Theseus, he covers it with his hand, and he cries. "Theseus, for a man like me, who was always known for being blessed, such change is unbearable." He is on his knees, his upper body covered in dried blood, his facial hair covered in tears and mucus. "For a man who always endured such a miserable life, a change would not bother him." He lets go of Theseus' hand. "Misery has always been a part of him." He stands, paces, and mumbles. "I think my misfortune will deliver me to the point where the earth will roar out to me, 'Do not touch my soil.'" He looks at the rubble that was Zeus' altar and cries. "The sea and the streams of all the rivers will say, 'I forbid you from crossing them.'" He stares at the bodies that were his family. "I shall become like the first men who shed kin blood, the Ixion, who are chained to a spinning wheel in the Underworld for all eternity." He weeps into his hands. "I once shared a joyful fortune with the Greeks, it would be best that I never be seen by them." He uncovers his face and screams into the heavens in the sky above. "What is the good of living such a useless and damned life?"

He finds a bench among the rubble that was his home and sits. He cries and mumbles into his hands. "Let gorgeous Hera blissfully dance, she has achieved her goal, and toppled the best of mortals right down to his foundations." He speaks into his hands and only he can understand his words. "What man would offer prayers to such a goddess? Her jealousy, born of her husband's visit to a mortal woman's bed, drives her to destroy an innocent man who has done humanity good." He wails into his hands and stops only to sniff then rub away the mucus that flows into his mustache.

Part VI: Exit in Health and a Healthy Entrance

My Plots of Land Are Your Plots of Land

Theseus looks at the pathetic specimen in front of him.

He was on his knees weeping and acting with shame. Like a woman! Who is this man? Where is the hero who saved me from the underworld below? Where is my friend?

Looking around the courtyard, he sees the old men. They talk and whisper while pointing at Hercules. He walks to the bench and stands in front of Hercules so the old men can't see him act so shamefully. He speaks in an even tone. "You are correct that this is Hera's work." He punches Hercules' shoulder. "But think carefully if this is your reason to die." He punches Hercules' chest. "Hercules, if I believed the gods cursed your life while providing every other mortal a life free of troubles then I would advise you to go ahead and die." He punches Hercules' chest. "But there's no mortal who hasn't been touched by misery." He slaps Hercules' face. "No god, either, if what the poets say is true." He bends down and speaks in a mocking tone. He holds up his fingers and begins counting. "Gods have gone to each other's bed," one, "committed sinful unions," two, "and, to become king, they fettered their fathers with shameful chains," three. He shrugs his shoulders. "Yet they still continue on with their sinful lives on Mount Olympus." He punches Hercules' chest. "Are you a mortal who judges sins more harshly than the gods?" He punches Hercules' chest and stands. "The gods see no wrong at all in their sin." He laughs.

He speaks in a voice loud enough so the old men behind and around him can hear. "Obey the law, Hercules. Leave Thebes and come with me to Athens. I will cleanse your hands of all blemishes, give you a home, and a portion of my wealth." He lifts Hercules off the bench and embraces him. He stands back, his upper body covered with Hercules' dried blood, and enjoys the memory of his friend. "When I killed the Knossos' Minotaur, and saved seven boys and seven, the Athenians gave me gifts."

He smiles, places his arm across Hercules' shoulder, and turns so they face the courtyard full of old men. His hoplites stand at attention. "The Athenians have given me countryside plots of land." He faces his hoplites. "While Hercules' lives, people will know that my plots of land are your plots of land." He walks with Hercules toward the hoplites. "Hercules, when you die and go to the Underworld, the whole of Athens will worship you as their hero with sacrifices and huge monuments." He has Hercules look at each hoplite in the eyes.

"In the eyes of Greeks, Athens will be a garland of achievement." He walks with Hercules around the courtyard so that Hercules has to face each of the old men. "All Greeks will speak well of Athena's city." He walks with Hercules to stand before Amphitryon. "The Greeks will praise Athens for performing a good deed to a hero such as Hercules."

He turns Hercules so they face one another. He speaks from his heart into Hercules' eyes. "This is how I will repay you for saving my life." He embraces Hercules. "I see that you are in need of friends." He rubs Hercules' back. "When the gods honor us with good fortune, Hercules, we do not need friends." He holds Hercules' shoulders, smiles, and gazes into his friend's eyes. "A god's help, if and when he chooses to give it, is enough." He embraces, and firmly holds onto, Hercules.

Hercules' eyes are wide and his speech is fast.

Oh Zeus, father in the sky above, thank you for bringing me such a friend as Theseus.

"Dear friend," he stands and rubs dried blood from his chest, "these things you said about the gods," he looks at his friend sternly, "are side issues and have nothing to do with my present troubles." He pulls his robe tightly so it covers his chest. "In any case, I don't believe that the gods engage in such unholy relationships." He walks toward the rubble that was Zeus' altar. "I have never believed, and I won't believe now, the story about gods tying up their parents in chains." He shakes his head. "I don't believe one god is the lord of another." He looks at Theseus. "A real god doesn't need anything." He looks into the sky above. "Poets invent miserable tales."

He paces the courtyard, makes eye contact with old men, speaks to Theseus, and mumbles to himself. "Though I'm still in misery, I have had a thought. If I kill myself, people might think I am a coward." He nods in agreement with himself. "If a man cannot stand against misfortune, how can he stand against an enemy's arrow?" He searches the courtyard for his bow, sees it lying on the ground underneath rubble that was once his home, and walks toward it. "I'll hold on to life and come with you to your city." He bends to pick up his bow. "I thank you profusely." He grabs his bow, stands erect, and smiles.

He wipes a tear from his eye and addresses the group of old men that surround the courtyard. "I have tasted pain and have rejected none." He remembers each of his labors, each heroic deed, and each heroic act that saved the city of Thebes. "I have shed no tears." He thinks about the absence of gratitude. "Nor did I think I ever would." He wipes eyes and draws his forearm over his mouth to wipe the mucus from his facial hair. "But now it seems I must be Fate's slave."

He turns toward Amphitryon. "Old father, I am now both murderer and exile." He walks to Amphitryon and embraces him. "Give my sons a proper burial." He holds onto his shoulder and looks into his eyes. "The law forbids me to put their burial clothes back on and shed a tear in their honor." He points toward the bodies that were his sons. "Let them lie against their mother's breast, in her arms, a communion of misery."

Walking toward the body that was his wife, he begins weeping. "Poor mother whom I unwittingly killed." Standing over the body that was his wife, he turns toward Amphitryon. "After the burial, stay in this city, father." Waving at the old men, he speaks consolingly. "It will not be easy but strengthen your heart to share in my misery."

Standing over the bodies that were his sons, he weeps. "My murdered sons." He stares at his eldest. "You have been deprived of your father's inheritance." He looks at his middle child. "You have been deprived of the great fame of my glorious labor." He looks at his youngest. "It would have been bestowed upon you had you lived."

Weeping, he walks toward his wife. "And you, my poor wife." He bends and leans over her body. "I killed you most unjustly." He weeps and shakes his head. "How unjustly I repaid you for your loyalty to our marriage bed and for watching over our household during my long absence." He leans over her body. "My poor wife, my poor sons, and poor me." He wipes his beard with his forearm. "Sweet pitiful kisses." He kisses her forehead.

He stands, bow in his right hand, and looks around the courtyard. His eyes stop at each of his arrows. "Should I keep my weapons or throw them away?" He walks around the courtyard mumbling. "If I wear them, they will dangle about my sides and call out, "We are the weapons you used to kill your wife and children." He mumbles, stoops, and grabs an arrow. "We are their murderers." Mumbling, he grabs an arrow. "'Why are you still holding on to us?'" Mumbling, he grabs an arrow. "How could I justify carrying them?" Mumbling, he grabs an arrow. "Should I strip myself of these weapons?" Mumbling, he grabs an arrow. "These weapons helped me perform glorious deeds throughout Greece." Mumbling, he grabs an arrow. "Should I get rid of my weapons and leave myself vulnerable to my enemies?" Mumbling, he grabs an arrow. "I will die a death of shame." Mumbling, he grabs an arrow. "No, I must keep my weapons and their misery." He searches the courtyard, sees he has grabbed all the arrows, counts the number in his quiver, then places the quiver over his shoulders.

Hercules stands. His robe is tied and his bloody chest is covered. He carries his bow and has a full quiver of arrows on his back. He smiles into the distance. Then he frowns and slumps his shoulders. He looks around the courtyard full of old men before settling on his friend. "Theseus, do me the favor of coming with me to Argos." He feels shame. "There is a reward I earned for bringing back that savage dog, Cerberus." He looks down at the dirt. "If you don't come with me, who knows what I might do on my own." He kicks the dirt. "My sadness for my sons might cause me to do some harm to myself." His eyes fill with tears and he cries.

He turns and looks at the old men standing around the courtyard. "Citizens of Thebes." He addresses each of them. "Cut off your hair." He speaks from his heart. "Join me in my mourning." He looks into their eyes. "Attend the burial of my sons." He places his hand on his chest. "Shed tears for all of us." He points at Amphitryon. "We have all been destroyed by Hera's cruel blow." He bows his head and cries.

I'll Lead The Way

Theseus walks toward his friend and embraces him. "Come, Hercules, you have shed enough tears." He motions for his hoplites.

Let's leave this place. I want my friend to return.

His friend won't move. "My limbs are frozen." Hercules weeps. "I can't leave this place."

Where is the man who brought me up from the underworld below?

The hoplites stand behind him. "Yes, Hercules. Misfortune overpowers even the mighty." He motions with his hand and they prepare to leave.

Hercules looks around the courtyard.

Come now. What is he looking at? This man is not the friend I know.

He hears Hercules whine, moan, and groan. "I wish I could turn into a rock." Hercules weeps. "I

want to be a rock, right here, upon this very spot."
Hercules moans and groans. "If I were a rock, I'd
remove the memory of my troubles." He weeps with
his hands in his face and rubs his forearm across his
beard.

Who is this wretched person? What a shameful
display!

Theseus walks to Hercules and slaps him across
the face. "Enough of this." He slaps Hercules with his
backhand. "Give your hand to a helping friend." He
reaches out to Hercules and offers his hand.

Hercules stands crumpled. He whines. "Take
care not to touch me." He pouts. "You don't want to
have this murder blood touch your clothes." He cries.

Where is the brave hero who saved me?

Theseus punches Hercules' chest and, when
Hercules doesn't respond, he punches again. He
punches and slaps Hercules. This goes on for minutes

until Hercules grabs his hand and gives him a fierce look.

Good! He's back.

Theseus smiles. "Hercules, let it be." He offers his hand in friendship. "Don't worry, I am not concerned." He pulls Hercules close and embraces him.

When he releases Hercules, they look into one another's eyes. He hears Hercules' grateful words. "Now that I have lost my sons, I shall regard you as a son." He feels a tear of happiness in his eyes.

He smiles and turns toward his hoplites. "Come, put your arm around my neck." He speaks to the old men in the courtyard. "I'll lead the way."

Hercules stands erect, wipes his beard with forearm, and tightens his robe. His smile fills Theseus' heart with happiness. "A pair of friends," his friend reaches out his hand, "one of which is wretched in his misery," he accepts it and pulls him forward for an embrace. His friend turns and faces Amphitryon.

"This is the sort of friend one ought to make, old

father."

Oh, Zeus! Thank you for letting me come here to

act and help my friend.

He grabs Hercules arms and the hoplites part so

the two can walk in front. He hears Amphitryon's

voice behind him. "The land that gave birth to

Hercules is a land that gives birth to good children."

Such Womanish Behavior

Hercules rubs his beard with his forearm, sniffs, and wipes his eyes with his fingers. He begins to walk away from the rubble that was his house but pauses. He inhales and stands erect. "Theseus, turn me around again. I want to see my sons once more."

His friend shakes his head and looks disappointed. "Do you think it will work like some soothing drug?"

I need to see them again. My poor sons will never experience the greatness of my name.

He feels the tears in his eyes, sniffs, and begins to cry. "I need to put my arms around my father."

"Here you are, son!" From behind, his father quickly embraces him. He feels his father's breath and Amphitryon leans against his back. "We both wish the same thing." Hercules turns and embraces his mortal father. They both weep.

He hears his friend speak with a very stern and disapproving tone. "Hercules, you performed all those glorious deeds." His friend pulls him away from his father's embrace. "Have you no memory of your labors?" His friend's tone is full of scorn and makes him feel shame.

Of course I remember! How could I forget my deeds?

His eyes flash with anger as he stares at his friend. "Those deeds caused me less hardship," he waves his hand at the bodies that were his family, "than do all these!" He weeps into his hands.

His friend's voice is angry and harsh which fills his heart with rage and shame. "Such womanish behavior." He sees his friend glance at the hoplites. "You won't be praised by anyone who sees you act like this." He narrows his eyebrows and glares.

Hercules faces his friend. "You think I lack nobility?" He punches Theseus in the chest. "Those weren't your words a moment ago." He prepares to strike Theseus again, but Theseus comes closer and embraces him.

Theseus speaks into Hercules' ear. "This is not noble behavior." He sees the hoplites and hears his friend's voice. "Where is the Hercules of the olden days?" His friend pushes him so they are face-to-face. His friend speaks loudly so the hoplites and old men can hear. "Where is the glorious Hercules?"

This is far too much! Has Theseus forgotten my deeds in the underworld? Has he lost his memory?

Hercules punches Theseus hard in the chest and then again in the stomach. The force causes Theseus to bend over. Hercules walks behind him, grabs his hair, and lifts Theseus' head so the hoplites can see his face. Hercules speaks to the hoplites. "Theseus, how did you behave when you were in the Underworld?"

Exactly. Let's Go.

Bent over from the force of Hercules' blow, Theseus begins laughing. He looks at the men in the hoplite line and laughs harder. He turns toward Hercules. "Even worse than you are now." Standing erect, he laughs and speaks directly to the men in the hoplites. "I acted worse than all men." He laughs and speaks so the old men in the courtyard can hear him. "I acted without courage." He continues laughing.

His friend looks at him with a bewildered expression. "Then how can you judge and say my troubles have removed my nobility?"

Theseus continues laughing, embraces his friend, and places his arm on his shoulder. He laughs and faces the hoplite men. "Exactly." His hand on Hercules' shoulder, he turns, faces his friend, and smiles. "Let's go." He gestures to the hoplites. "Let's leave for the city of Athena."

He, his friend, and the group of hoplites begin walking down the hill and toward the Athenian encampment. Hercules pauses and turns toward Amphitryon. "Farewell, old father."

Spoken with sadness but without shame.

Amphitryon looks at Hercules with eyes that say he knows he'll never see his son again.

He deserves pity. The gods did not smile on Amphitryon.

Amphitryon waves his hand. "And to you too, my son."

The group continues down the hill when Hercules shouts. "Bury my sons as I asked, father."

Part VII: The Disease Remains

But How?

Amphitryon takes his cane and walks toward the path leading down the hill. "And me?" He looks at the back of Hercules' head. "Who will bury me, my son?"

Hercules continues down the path and speaks without turning his head. "I will, father."

He stares at the back of Hercules' disappearing head and speaks loudly. "When will you come back?"

His son is out of sight but he can hear Hercules' voice. "After your death, father."

He leans on his cane and shouts. "But how?"

His son is out of sight and he can only make out parts of Hercules' speech as they descend down the hill. "Father, I... bring you..Athens...sad burden....my sons...shameful destroyer...follow Theseus like a boat in tow....wealth or power...good friends think wrong."

Amphitryon stands in the middle of the courtyard surrounded by the rubble that was Hercules' home and the bodies that were Hercules' family. He stares at the twenty old men, falls to his knees, covers his face with his hands, and cries.

After minutes, he hears the old captain speak. "Let us leave this place in pity and grief."

His old sergeant quickly agrees. "We will leave full of tears and sadness."

He hears his twenty old friends leave and walk down the path. He hears the sentence, "We have lost our greatest friend," and then their voices disappear as they walk toward the city of Thebes.

End of Euripides' "Hercules"